BATTLE BUGS

THE DRAGONFLY DEFENSE

BATTLE BUGS

THE DRAGONFLY DEFENSE

by **JACK PATTON**
illustrated by **BRETT BEAN**

SCHOLASTIC INC.

With special thanks to Adrian Bott

Text copyright © 2016 by Hothouse Fiction.
Cover and interior art by Brett Bean, copyright © 2016 by Scholastic Inc.

All rights reserved. Published by Scholastic Inc., *Publishers since 1920*, 557 Broadway, New York, NY 10012, by arrangement with Hothouse Fiction. Series created by Hothouse Fiction.

ISBN 978-0-545-94509-7

10 9 8 7 6 5 4 3 2 1   16 17 18 19 20

Printed in the U.S.A.   40
First printing 2016
Book design by Phil Falco and Ellen Duda

CONTENTS

DRAGONFLY'S WARNING

Max Darwin woke up with a jolt. A deep rattling, gurgling noise was coming from overhead.

The thought hit him: *I'm back on Bug Island! A giant lizard's about to swallow me whole!*

Max sat bolt upright and opened his eyes.

He looked around, saw the timber walls and the bunk beds in the dim morning light from the shuttered window, and remembered where he was.

This wasn't Bug Island at all. It was the boys' cabin at Camp Greenwood. The noise he could hear was Scott Downie in the bunk above, snoring. Although the sound was gross and very loud, somehow all the other boys were still fast asleep.

Max lay back down with a sigh. Camp had been awesome so far. There had been boating, archery, science projects with microscopes, and a whole LOT of bug hunting. As cool as camp was, it couldn't quite match the thrill of battling alongside the intelligent, talking bugs of Bug Island. After two weeks of summer camp, he was starting to miss his home and his bug collection, too. His mom sent him daily texts telling him they were all fine, but he still wanted to see for himself.

That reminded him. There was something he had to do. Something he did every day, while the other kids were still asleep, or whenever he could grab a moment to himself.

"Time to check the encyclopedia," he whispered to himself. "Just in case . . ."

He groped under his bed and found the thick, heavy *The Complete Encyclopedia of Arthropods*. The magical book was a priceless collection of bug knowledge, but also a magical gateway. Whenever it glowed with a special light, Max knew he'd be able to travel through its pages to Bug Island.

When he saw there was no telltale glow coming from the pages, he was disappointed but not surprised. *I guess the bugs don't need me anymore*, he thought sadly.

Still, he flipped through the pages eagerly until he reached the double-page map of Bug Island. The book must have had *some* strange magic left in it, because the map had updated itself after his last visit. The lava bridge that had connected Reptile Island to Bug Island was gone now, and only a few rocky islets were left where it had once been.

Max remembered how the lava bridge had been the cause of a long, bitter war between the bugs and the reptiles, which the bugs had eventually won. The bridge had been smashed away by a gigantic wave—a wave that had taken General Komodo with it. The bugs had defeated the reptiles once and for all, and Bug Island was safe. Forever.

I'm glad, Max thought. *But I sure do miss the adventure.*

Just then, Scott Downie let out an ear-splitting snore like a hippo gargling with mud. Across the room, Jamal Peters sat up and rubbed his eyes sleepily. "Scott, you're going to wake the whole camp!"

Max quickly hid the encyclopedia under his covers before Jamal could see it.

There was a knock at the door. The friendly voice of Joe the camp counselor rang out: "Rise and shine, folks! Last day today. That means you get to do whatever you want."

All around, boys stirred and stretched. "River trip!" Mark Garcia yelled, bounding out of bed. "Last one to breakfast is a toad's butt. Go!"

Max got dressed and washed as quickly as he could, then rushed to breakfast at the main lodge. He didn't care about being a toad's butt, but he did want to get down to the river.

Together with the other boys, he wolfed down cereal, eggs, toast, and orange juice before charging out into the late-summer warmth.

Mark Garcia was already there, grinning and waiting for them all. "Ready for this?"

"You know it!" Max laughed.

"Okay! Let's hit that jetty. Last one in the water is a—hey, Max, I never said 'go!'"

Max was already on his way to the water, his arms and legs pumping.

He sprinted down the dusty track that led the way through the woods. The other boys came storming up behind him, yelling. Up ahead, he could see the river glittering through the trees in the sunlight.

He was in the lead! He sped up his pace, edging out the other boys, keeping the wooden jetty fixed in his view. No stopping now. He was going to run all the way to the end of the jetty—and right off it!

His feet pounded the path. The jetty loomed up ahead. The way was clear. Only a few yards more to go.

Then a bright yellow flash on the riverbank caught his eye.

Instantly, he knew what it was: a dragonfly, perched on a log. Nothing unusual about that . . .

But then, it shot into the air, flew up and down in an odd, jerky zigzag, then settled back down again.

Max stopped in his tracks. There was definitely something weird about *that*.

The other boys swerved past him, but he

just had to stop and stare at the dragonfly. *What's it doing?* he thought.

Again, the dragonfly flew up and did its strange flight routine. Up-down-up-down, left to right, then settle.

The boys splashed in the river, whooping and throwing water at one another. Mark Garcia whooshed past Max and leaped in. "Too slow!" he yelled as he cannonballed into the water.

Max ignored him. Something about the dragonfly's behavior was—well— *bugging* him.

It did the midair dance again, and suddenly Max knew what he was looking at.

"It's a letter M," he said, amazed.

Jamal Peters swam up to the jetty and squinted at Max. "You coming?"

"Just got to get my magnifying glass," Max replied. "I need a closer look at that bug!"

"You're bug crazy!" Jamal laughed.

Max began to race back to the cabin, but a droning noise followed him as he went. He glanced behind and saw that the dragonfly was following him.

Wild excitement gripped him. He wasn't imagining this.

The moment he burst through the cabin door, he saw light shining from under his bed. Only one thing gave off that unearthly, silvery glow: the encyclopedia!

Max quickly changed his clothes. He yanked the encyclopedia open, found the magnifying glass, and held it over the map. In an instant the dragonfly shot over his shoulder and dived into the book. Max watched it grow tiny until it vanished from sight.

Then a strong, familiar feeling tugged at him. A breeze ruffled his hair, growing stronger and stronger until it was a gale. A poster was ripped off the cabin wall.

Max laughed out loud as he was pulled off his feet into the open pages, into the whirling funnel of wind between the worlds.

Here I go! he thought. *Back to Bug Island!*

STORM IS COMING

Max dropped out of the cloudy sky above Bug Island. He smacked straight into a thick green leaf, tumbled off it, then fell and landed on another one. He continued, leaf after leaf, until he finally came to rest in a tangle of vines.

Once he was sure which way was up, he took a look around. He'd fallen down the length of a gigantic tree. The leaves on its branches had, fortunately, slowed him down.

There were more huge trees close by. Their thick trunks rose like skyscrapers into the misty gloom overhead. The air was moist, and droplets of water hung from the leaves.

"I must be in the rain forest," Max said to himself. "And I'm lost. As usual!"

Max glanced around to see if any of his bug friends were nearby. There was no sign of any of them. Well, that wasn't unusual. Most times when he'd come to Bug Island before, he'd dropped down somewhere random—or dangerous—and had to hunt for them.

What *was* unusual was how dark it was here. Back in the human world, it had been sunny and bright, but there were black clouds over Bug Island. It felt like a heck of a storm was on the way. He hoped the dragonfly that led him here had made it to shelter.

The dragonfly! It had flown through to Bug Island with him. *That had never happened before!* He stretched in his cradle of vines, looking all over, but there was no sign of the bright yellow insect.

From above came a low, distant rumble of thunder.

"Time to get moving!" Max said to himself. Not only was the sky threatening to erupt, something about the forest was giving him the creeps.

He tugged himself free from the tree vines and scrambled down a long, sloping root until he reached the forest floor. He walked across decaying, fallen leaves that were squishy and crumbly, like moldy old mattresses. He quickly learned to keep his feet on only the newest, firmest leaves.

Up ahead, he could see light through the gloomy trees—he hoped it was some kind of clearing. He hurried toward it, bounding from one leaf to the next.

Directly in his path lay a stretch of boggy ground. The marshy black earth didn't look safe, so he had to clamber up and onto a fallen branch. Although it was only a branch, it felt like a tree to bug-sized Max.

As he struggled to climb up it, something below him made a rustling sound, and the bright reflection of eyes peered out from the undergrowth.

Uh-oh, he thought. *I'm being watched!*

Max felt a surge of fear. He heaved himself up on top of the branch. The leaves were moving. Something big was pushing through underneath them and it was coming his way!

Max let out a yell and slid down the other side of the branch. The marshy mud slurped up over his ankles, but he didn't care. He pulled himself free and ran for his life.

The whatever-it-was behind him was still coming. Max could hear the *whish-whish-whish* of something large scurrying through the moldy leaves. He ran for the light ahead, praying it would mean shelter.

The next moment, he burst through the trees and ran out into the lit-up clearing. He stared at the amazing sight before him, then laughed in delight.

The Battle Bug camp!

But instead of the half-smashed, messy, thrown-together camp he remembered, this was a mighty, walled stockade, more like a medieval fortress. Bugs were trooping back and forth on the outermost battlements. Waiting there in the main archway was a group of bugs Max knew very well indeed: Buzz the hornet, Webster the trap-door spider, and Barton the titan beetle!

"Battle Bugs!" he yelled. "It's me! Max!"

They all turned to look at him. Max stopped in his tracks. The bugs looked totally surprised. It was as if they weren't expecting him at all.

"MAX!" they chorused in unison.

A twig snapped behind him. Max spun around—and the *thing* from the forest loomed up in front of him . . .

"Spike!"

"It *is* you, short stuff!" yelled Spike the emperor scorpion. "You're back!"

"I don't believe it!" Max said, relieved. "What were you doing out there in the forest? I thought you were a lizard."

"I thought *you* were a lizard!" Spike said. "I was on forest patrol and I heard something crashing through the leaves making *tons* of noise, so I thought I'd better check it out."

"No harm done," Max said, giving Spike a friendly pat as they made their way toward the other bugs.

"What's the problem this time?" he called out.

"Problem?" Buzz looked blank.

"The emergency," Max said.

"Emergency?" Webster repeated.

"You know . . . the reason I've been called back to Bug Island!"

The bugs looked at one another, puzzled.

"We have no idea," Barton said.

Max sighed. Something very weird was

going on—there had *always* been a reason the book had called him back to Bug Island.

Max and the bugs trooped to the top of the tower in the midst of the new camp. There were many new bugs since his last visit. They had never seen a human being before. Thousands of bugs watched in fascination as he passed by.

"You're all surprised to see me?" he asked his friends.

"We are!" whispered shy Webster. "Normally I don't like surprises, but it *is* good to have you back."

"You haven't seen any lizards lately?"

"No one's seen a lizard for ages," said Buzz. "We run regular patrols. Everything's quiet. We haven't spotted so much as a newt."

"I wonder why that dragonfly called me, then?" Max asked.

"What dragonfly?" asked Spike, rubbing his shiny head in confusion.

"A yellow one. It was trying to get my attention over in my world. And it flew through to Bug Island ahead of me, which has never happened before. I thought something was really wrong!"

"Maybe it was just a mistake," Buzz said, shrugging her stripy thorax.

"Even if it was, I'm not complaining!" Max said. "This new camp you've built is amazing!"

"It's good to live in peace for once," Webster said. "We're all having a great time."

"Well . . . maybe not *all* of us," Buzz said.

They all looked over to where General Barton stood quietly in the corner.

"Don't mind me," he muttered. "I'm just a general without an army to command."

"Between you and me," Webster whispered in Max's ear, "I think he feels like the bugs don't need him anymore."

"Of course they do!" Max whispered back. He looked over at Barton.

Just as Max was trying to think of something to make Barton feel better, a tremendous crash of thunder shook the clearing. A fat glob of rain fell, and then another, bursting like a bombshell only a few feet away.

A rainstorm when you were bug-sized was serious business. Max and the bugs weren't just at risk of getting wet. The raindrops were hitting like cannonballs, hammering down all around!

Suddenly, Barton sprang into action. "Take cover!" he shouted.

MAX TO THE RESCUE

Barton snapped into action mode. He scrambled to a platform on the edge of the tower and shouted down to the assembled bugs:

"Everybody get under cover, NOW! All flying bugs, land immediately!"

A boulder-sized raindrop smashed down on top of Barton's thick body armor, flattening the general. He struggled back to his feet as Max rushed over to make sure he was all right.

"I'm fine!" Barton gasped, wobbling slightly. "I just need to make sure all the bugs get to shelter."

"I'll take charge of the ground bugs," Max said. "Spike, Webster, Barton, you take the rest to safety!"

"You got it!" Spike bellowed. He and Webster and Barton raced into the tunnels inside the main tower.

Max ran to the perch Barton had used and looked out over the rain-drenched camp.

Ranks of beetles, ants, and spiders all scurried around in chaos, trying to avoid the raindrops. Bugs were flung about in the wind as gusts swept through the camp.

"Keep moving!" Max yelled.

Then he heard a cry from below. One of the smaller ant sentries had been knocked off her lookout post by the wind. She flew through the air like a leaf and fell into a small hole on the battlements. She squirmed about helplessly, unable to get back on her feet.

"Hang in there, soldier," Max cried above the wind. "I'm coming for you!" The other Battle Bugs were helping get the camp's occupants under cover—it was up to him to do something. If the rainwater filled up the hole the ant had fallen into, she would drown.

He sprinted from the central tower across a bridge made from wasp's nest material. He dodged out of the way of falling raindrops that exploded like bomb blasts. The raindrops had torn a giant hole in the bridge. There was no way for Max to get to the ant now!

"Help!" the ant cried in a wheezy voice.

Max raced back the way he came, looking for another way over to the ant. A tangle of vines snaked above him. Suddenly he had an idea.

If I can just reach, Max thought. *Then maybe I don't need the bridge at all!*

Max jumped and just managed to grab on to one of the vines with his fingertips. He yanked down until one side of the vine came loose. He stood on the edge of the battlement and took aim at the ant.

I hope this works, he thought.

With a whooping noise like Tarzan, he gripped the vine tight and leaped from the tower.

"Incoming!" he yelled. "Grab on!"

As the vine swung over, he clung to it with his right hand and reached out with his left. In one smooth motion he grabbed the stranded ant and swung back to the other side.

"Gotcha!" he cried, depositing the ant safely on dry land.

"Thanks!" she cried. She saluted and headed off to help evacuate more bugs underground.

Suddenly, Webster popped out of one of the tower doors.

"M-Max," he stammered. "We've got incoming!"

"What is it, Webster?" Max asked frantically. "Not a lizard?"

"N-no—it's one of ours!" Webster replied.

Max looked up into the stormy sky. A droning noise from above caught his attention. It was growing louder and louder, spiraling out of control in the blustery winds, trying to dodge the raindrops. He looked up and saw a winged insect coming in fast, rolling and tumbling in the air.

"Slow down!" he yelled at it. He waved his arms frantically. "You're coming in way too fast! You're going to crash—"

The creature barreled right into Max. Its long body turned too late to avoid him and knocked him sprawling, right over the tower ledge.

Max caught the ledge with one flailing hand and sank his fingers deep into the damp, termite-chewed clay. His heart pounding, he pulled himself back up and glared at the bug, which was now perched on all its legs.

"Careful!" he yelled. "I almost went over!"

His voice died away as he realized what he was looking at. The insect was bright yellow and had a big, bulbous head and great shimmering wings. It was a dragonfly—an Australian emperor, by the

look of her. And though he couldn't have said why, Max was certain she was the same dragonfly he'd seen by the river back in the human world.

"I'm really sorry," the dragonfly said. "My wings gave out on me as I was coming in to land. The rain has soaked them through. My name is Spotter, by the way. You must be the Max I've heard so much about."

Max nodded, still a little breathless from his near fall.

"I need to talk to you, urgently. Barton, too."

Max hurried her down the tunnel into the shelter of the inner chambers. Barton, Spike, and the others were gathered in a domed room. Bugs clung to the walls and ceiling, sheltering from the rain. The glowing bodies of fireflies lit the room with a soft, crimson light, reminding Max of emergency lighting when the power goes off.

"Spotter!" Barton cried. "One of my best reconnaissance bugs. Glad to see you made it through the storm."

"I'm afraid I have bad news, General," the dragonfly said. "I was on patrol over Darkmist Lagoon below Eternity Falls, when I saw something I never expected to see again."

All the bugs listened in fearful silence.

Spotter went on: "I saw them clear as day—lizards!"

At the word *lizards*, the bugs went crazy. Buzzes, clicks, whirrs, and squeaks of alarm went up. Grasshoppers rebounded off the walls and wood lice instantly rolled up in balls. The racket completely drowned out what Spotter was saying.

"QUIET!" Barton roared.

The room fell silent again.

"Lizards?" Barton repeated, aghast.

"That's impossible!" Spike added.

"We defeated them!" Buzz protested.

"And the lava bridge was de-de-destroyed!" Webster stammered.

"I know what I saw," Spotter said. "A group of lizards, gathered at the water's edge. And I knew I had to act fast. I had to tell Max. So I flew up into the sky and just kept going. Eventually I broke through into the amazing place where Max comes from!"

Max was astonished. "If there are lizards at Darkmist Lagoon, that means they've somehow found a way back onto Bug Island. We have to do something."

"Yes we do, my human friend," Barton said. "I propose we assemble a group of water-based insects to check out the sighting."

"Got any particular bugs in mind?" Max asked.

"I do," Barton said, "First Officer Hawthorn, present arms!"

In an instant, a platoon of shield bugs stood before Barton.

"His troops can walk on water, as well as being fierce fighters with strong defenses. Isn't that right, Hawthorn?"

"Sir, yes, sir!" rasped Hawthorn.

"Bring it on!" hollered the shield bugs.

Max nodded. Like Barton, these bugs had clearly been itching for something to do. Well, now their wish would be granted.

"Right. The storm has died down. Time to move out. Ready to get the old double act back together, Spike?" Max asked.

"Anytime!" said Spike. He lowered his head so that Max could climb up. Max sat on Spike's back, riding him like a trusty warhorse.

With Barton leading the way, Spotter in the air, and the shield bugs marching in formation close behind, the expedition set off for the lagoon. Nobody spoke a word. Max could tell they were all thinking about what they might find: If the lizards were back, then so was the war!

LAGOON LIZARDS

The rain was still falling, but now it was only a light mist. The bug expedition wasn't in danger now—not from the rain, anyway—but it did make the forest feel spooky and gloomy. As Max and Spike followed Barton through the jungle foliage, a rich smell rose up from all around them.

Spike, usually brave and tough, was

worried. "What if the lizards *have* come back, Max? What are we gonna do?"

"We beat them once," Max reminded him. "We can do it again."

"But what if it's a new sort of lizard? With wings? And it breathes fire?"

Max laughed. "Then we'll just have to use new tactics. And we might need a fire extinguisher."

"Keep quiet!" Barton snapped. "If those scaly creeps really are back on our island, we don't want to let them know we're coming!"

Spike fell silent.

The expedition plodded over bulging tree roots and around moss-covered rocks that loomed overhead like the ruins of ancient castles. Not one bug made a sound, except for the faint drone of Spotter's wings from above.

"This is a fool's errand," grumbled First Officer Hawthorn. "I bet that dragonfly didn't even see any lizards."

"If Spotter says she saw lizards, then I believe her," Max said.

Soon, in the distance, Max caught the sound of rushing, churning water.

Eternity Falls, he thought. *We're nearly at the lagoon*.

Sure enough, he saw the glint of water through the trees. The group silently approached in the shadow of the forest, until Barton signaled them to stop. "Any farther and we'll be seen," he warned.

Max looked out across the broad lagoon, all the way to the trees on the far side. The waterfall crashed and roared, sending spray up into the air.

Then he caught sight of something that chilled his blood. Up ahead, at the water's edge, three smooth, green lizards crept slowly along. They glanced all around with beady little eyes.

"It's true," he whispered. "They're back!"

"Is that it? Only three?" Barton rumbled.

Max was puzzled. This wasn't some terrifying new lizard troop. They were just common lizards—definitely a threat, but hardly a deadly one.

They were muttering to one another as they walked. Max couldn't hear a word because of the thundering waterfall. He watched them from the shadows and tried to figure out what they were doing.

"I think they're scoping the area out, Barton," he whispered.

Barton nodded. "You're right. But for what?"

"Let's get a little closer, Spike," said Max. "Keep your tail down. They might see it poking out from the leaves."

Spike obediently tucked his segmented tail down. Together, they moved stealthily through the foliage.

Max could hear their hissing voices, but he still couldn't quite make out the words. He strained to catch what the lizards were saying. One of them said something like "landing."

Then an angry bellow from the forest startled him. It was First Officer Hawthorn. "I've had about enough of this skulking!" the bug raged. "I'm not letting a bunch of lizards wander around the lagoon on my watch."

"NOO!" Max shouted. "Wait!"

It was too late; First Officer Hawthorn readied his troops. "Shield bugs," he screamed, "CHARGE!"

The three lizards looked up, taken completely by surprise. A brown wall of shield bugs was bearing down on them through the mist, galloping out of the forest like a cavalry charge.

"So much for stealth," Spike said.

The shield bugs slammed into the lizards, bowling them over and sending them sprawling in the wet mulch. One of them toppled over the edge of the lagoon and fell in with a plop.

Glaring, the other two lizards rolled back onto their feet. They launched a vicious counterattack, clawing and snapping at the bugs.

The shield bugs really did look like shields; they had broad, tough backs protecting them from attacks from above and in front. In a group, they were like Roman legionnaires, with their shield-like bodies forming a turtle-shaped mass.

First Officer Hawthorn clambered onto

his own troops' backs and scurried across them so he could jab a lizard on the nose with his pointy mouthparts.

"That trigger-happy bug's wrecked the whole plan!" Max grumbled. "Come on, Spike. We may as well join the attack now!"

Max and Spike galloped into the fight, coming at the lizards from the side. The lizards had no idea they had been hiding so close by, and Spike's powerful charge came as a total surprise. He struck with his stinger, injuring one of the lizards and narrowly missing another.

The lizard who had fallen into the lagoon came slithering back out, dripping wet and furious. "Stand your ground, fools! Pick those bugs off one by one."

One of the lizards grabbed a shield bug in his mouth and flung him into the lagoon, where he landed on his back and started to float away like a stray leaf, kicking his legs angrily.

"Now the scorpion," hissed the lizard leader. "He's the most dangerous of the group. Take him down."

The lizards rushed at Spike, ducking under his pincers and shoving him with their blunt heads. "Turn him over!" the leader yelled. "He can't use that stinger if he's on his back."

Spike rolled back and forth like a boat in a storm as the lizards tried to upend him. The shield bugs nipped and scratched at the lizards, but the advantage of surprise was gone and they couldn't do much to hurt them.

Up on Spike's back, Max fought to keep control. It was impossible. The mist was making Spike's plating slippery, and Max had nothing to hang on to. The lizards shoved, Spike reared up, and Max went tumbling off his back.

"Argh!" he yelled as he landed hard on the muddy ground.

Max struggled to his feet. His hands, knees, and face were plastered with wet mud. It was hard to see through the haze of rain, but he could make out Spike's huge form grabbing at the angry lizards. "Max?" Spike bellowed. "Where'd you go, little buddy?"

"Over here!" Max yelled. He ran in Spike's direction, but an ugly sight lunged into his path.

It was the injured lizard, the one Spike had stung. Half its face was swollen and it squinted at him through one open eye. "You're not going *anywhere*," it slobbered, its fat tongue lolling out of its mouth.

Max had no choice. He turned and ran.

The lizard came hobbling after him. Spike's venom was slowing it down, but not by much. Max darted this way and that, but the lizard was on him at every turn.

He desperately looked around for some- where safe to run. To his horror he realized the lizard had chased him right up to the brim of the lagoon. All this drizzly mist was making it hard to see where he was going. If he tried to swim, the lizard would snap him up for sure.

Then he saw a fallen tree branch overhanging the water. The lizard lunged suddenly, missing Max by mere inches.

There was nowhere else to go. Max clambered up the branch, the slimy wood leaving brown patches on his palms. He felt the branch wobble beneath him and knew the lizard was still in pursuit. It had climbed onto the branch behind him!

I'm really in trouble now, he thought. Spike was nowhere in sight.

He retreated farther up the branch, which dangled above the water and sagged alarmingly under his feet. The grinning lizard advanced on him, shuffling forward on its belly. With its one good eye and its evil leer, it made Max think of a pirate. *And I'm walking the plank!*

He looked down into the water and wondered if he should jump. It was a long way to fall, and he couldn't tell what might be lurking in those depths.

Thunder rumbled. The lizard was almost upon him. It opened its red mouth, yawning wide, showing rows of sharp teeth. Max shrank back as far as he dared, onto the last precious few steps of the branch.

A brilliant white flash lit the sky. Lightning arced down into the branch they were clinging to. There was a groan, a splintering sound, and a sickening crack.

Max stared in horror and saw the blackened, smoldering wood where the lightning had struck. The branch broke with a sudden snap, and fell. Max went tumbling into the waiting waters of the lagoon.

INTO THE RAPIDS

The water of Darkmist Lagoon was shockingly cold. Max fought not to panic. He'd dive-bombed into water dozens of times back at camp. He just had to stay calm and remember what to do.

He swam hard for the surface. In the murky underwater light he saw the long, dark shape of the smashed-off branch sinking down and down. There was no sign of the lizard that had been chasing him. Max hoped it wasn't ready to swim up and bite his ankles.

He broke the surface and took a deep gasp of air. On the shore, the Battle Bugs were still fighting the remaining lizards. He shouted for help but his calls were lost on the wind.

He tried to swim back, but suddenly he realized he was being pulled away by the powerful current. The force of the waterfalls flowing into Darkmist Lagoon was creating an underwater pull that was sweeping him out of the bay and toward the river.

"Max!" yelled Spotter the dragonfly.

"Keep your head above water. I'm coming to get you!"

She zoomed toward him, flying low above the water like a rescue helicopter. Max battled the water, pumping his arms and legs, but he was caught in the current's grip and picking up speed.

He felt the gust from Spotter's fast-beating wings on his face as she came in for the rescue. Max reached out a grateful hand, and she dipped down so she could bring her legs within reach.

"Grab on! I'll carry you!"

"I'm trying!" Max gasped as his out-stretched hand brushed one of her legs. He tried to grab it, but a surge of water dragged him under again. He could still hear her muffled cries as the current swept him out of the lagoon and into the faster-flowing section of the river.

"Spotter? Where are you?" he yelled as he kicked his way to the surface again.

Max gasped and puffed as the icy water of the river swirled around him. The lagoon continually emptied itself into the narrow waterway, which made for a fast-flowing river. Max struggled to swim for the bank, but the current was just too strong. At camp they would have warned him not to try going down it in a canoe, let alone try to swim in it without a life jacket!

He tumbled and twisted as the river rushed between rocks. The shore was way out of reach. Fragments of twig, broken off when the lightning struck the branch, swept past him and away.

He caught a glimpse of what lay ahead. "Oh, no!" He gasped. The river was anything but gentle. It foamed and roared, with jagged chunks of rock sticking up like icebergs. "I'm heading into rapids!"

Max had to do something or he'd be smashed on the rocks like a bug on a windshield. An idea flashed into his mind. If he could find something to hang on to, he might be able to keep his head above water. He lunged for one of the bits of branch as it rushed past.

"Gotcha!" he cried. He wrapped his arms around it and clung on for dear life.

The rapids swallowed Max up and he

was hurled into a nightmare of surging foam, looming rock faces, and plunge after plunge into deep water. He had barely enough time to fill his lungs before he went under again.

The last time he'd been through anything like this, it was the log flume ride at his favorite theme park—only that had been *fun*, not deadly. His knuckles were white and his fingers numb with cold, but he still hung on. Slowly, the torrent became a flow, which became a gentle wash. Max kicked his legs and found he could dog paddle toward the shore.

At last.

Max let go of the twig and pulled himself out onto the sandy bank. For a moment he

just lay there, dazed and soaked to the skin. The warm sunlight felt good on his face.

Wait. Sunlight?

He got to his feet and looked around. The storm had passed and the sun was streaming down through a ragged gap in the clouds. There was no more mist.

"Well," he said to himself, breathing hard, "I may be soaking wet and miles away from the other bugs, but I guess things could be a lot worse!"

If he was ever going to find his way back to the bug camp, he had to get his bearings. Max took a good long look around, checking out the environment.

The river had washed him into a gorge. The muddy riverbanks stretched for only a little way before large, rocky cliffs rose on either side. It was like being at the bottom of the Grand Canyon.

"I've seen this place on the map," he said to himself. "It must be Flintfang Gorge!"

Max thought about trying to return the way he'd come, but decided against it. There was no way he could struggle against the water's flow, and besides, there might be more lizards that way. He didn't really like the idea of going back into the river and heading downstream, either.

The only other way out of here was to climb up the cliffs. They looked pretty steep, and not at all safe.

Max stared at their loose, crumbly surfaces, and wished—not for the first time—that he could just turn into a many-legged bug and go scampering up them easily.

"Anyone up there?" he shouted. "Spike? Buzz? Spotter?"

No answer came.

Max heaved a sigh and trudged toward the bottom of the cliff. Then he spotted something that made his heart thump like a deathwatch beetle.

Tracks in the mud. Deep, dragging ones, left by something huge. He couldn't tell what kind of creature it was, but he knew for sure it wasn't a bug.

"That settles it," Max announced. "I'm getting up those cliffs and out of here!"

Feeling determined, Max began to climb. He made it up about a fifth of the way before the rock he was putting his weight on tore free. He went skidding down the side with a yell.

Max picked himself up, brushed off the dirt, took a deep breath, and tried again.

His second attempt was even worse than the first. A chunk of flint gave way under his foot. Max slid all the way down, yelling, as the rocky surface broke apart like so much loose dirt. A fat boulder that looked like something left over from Stonehenge came rolling down toward him. Max struggled to his feet and dived out of the way—not quite fast enough.

The boulder came to rest on top of him, pressing his leg painfully down into the mud. A forceful tug told him he was stuck tight.

"Oh, *great*!" he yelled. "Can this day get any worse?"

Suddenly a dark shadow appeared above him, and two rows of jagged teeth came into view. There was no mistaking the great, brutish power of what was staring down at him: a huge saltwater crocodile.

"Oh, I think things can get much worse," it hissed in glee.

LONGTOOTH TROUBLE

Max wriggled and tugged for all he was worth, fighting to pull his leg out from under the rock.

The crocodile slid its gigantic bulk toward him. It was in no hurry. Its clawed feet gouged deep trenches in the mud as it went. There was no doubting what had made those tracks now.

"Stuck, are you?" The crocodile smirked. "I wouldn't worry about it. Struggling isn't going to do you any good."

"I guess the volcano missed a few of you reptiles," Max snapped back bravely.

He hoped talking tough would make him feel tough, because right now he was so terrified he could hardly think. The crocodile was the length of an express train to him, and its head the size of a bus. He'd never seen a monster like it.

The crocodile gave a throaty laugh. "I'd heard you were a gutsy one! Tell you what, I'll finish you off really fast." It snapped its jaws and slid a little closer. Max saw a jagged scar across its nose, where something must have hurt it badly long ago.

"You don't scare me!" Max shouted, and tugged at his leg again.

Fresh hope gripped him as his ankle slid a little way out from under the rock.

"Why, I'm forgetting my manners," leered the crocodile. "I haven't introduced myself. I'm General Longtooth. I believe you ran into my troop up at the lagoon."

"Those common lizards?" Max scoffed. "They didn't give us any trouble."

General Longtooth's head loomed over him, blocking out the sky. Max heaved himself backward and dragged his foot out a little farther. Only the rubber sole of his sneaker was catching now.

"You'll have plenty of trouble soon enough!" roared General Longtooth. "Once the crocodile fleet makes it over from Reptile Island, your bug friends will be antenna-deep in trouble! The reptiles are coming back, and there's nothing anyone can do to stop us!"

Max put two and two together in his mind, and suddenly he understood everything. Crocodiles were aquatic. And they were big enough to carry other reptiles. A lizard armada was coming, attacking by *water* this time, not by land. The crafty reptiles had found a way to reach Bug Island even without the lava bridge!

"We already stopped you. General Komodo and his troops were destroyed by the tsunami. The war is over and your side lost." Max's leg was almost free now. Just one more heave ought to do it . . .

Longtooth peered down the length of his scaly snout at Max. "Really, I should thank you. With Komodo gone, I finally get to be in charge!"

The massive jaws gaped wide. Longtooth lunged at Max.

Max scrabbled backward as far as he could. His foot was still stuck. Thinking quickly, he grabbed a stone. As the monstrous head plunged down to devour him, Max flung the stone squarely at Longtooth's glaring eye.

The stone hit home. Longtooth reared up and cried out in pain. So, it was true—the crocodile's eye really was its most vulnerable spot!

While the enormous reptile thrashed in agony, Max gave a final desperate heave and wrestled his trapped foot out from under the rock. It hurt like wildfire, but he forced himself to his feet and ran.

"Get back here!" roared Longtooth. "Where do you think you're going?"

Max ran. Behind him, he heard the ghastly, slithering thumps of Longtooth's feet slapping on the ground as the crocodile gave chase. The riverbank mud sucked at Max's feet, slowing him down, and his ankle burned with pain.

A monster's chasing me and I can't run. It's like being trapped in a nightmare!

His only chance was to run to a loose pile of rocks up ahead and try to hide among them. The crocodile's vast size might work against it. But as he ran, with Longtooth's jaws snapping behind him, he knew he'd never make it. He kept stumbling and tripping on his injured leg, and every time, the crocodile gained some ground. He could hear its wheezing breath over his shoulder.

Then, from high overhead, came a droning noise. It was getting louder. Hardly daring to hope, Max glanced up and saw a welcome flash of yellow.

"Spotter!"

"Coming in for immediate evac!" yelled Spotter.

Max kept running for the rock heap. Instead of diving in among the rocks as he'd planned to, he leaped up one rock after another until he was poised at the very top.

General Longtooth roared like a tyrannosaur and lunged again.

Max jumped at the very last moment. He caught hold of Spotter's body with his outstretched arms, and though the dragonfly swerved and wobbled in the air, she stayed airborne.

"Hang on!" she yelled, her wings as loud as a propeller. "We're getting out of here."

As Spotter flew full tilt up and away, Longtooth heaved himself up onto the rock pile and aimed one last vicious snap at Max.

The jaws clashed shut right under Max's dangling laces. He could smell Longtooth's foul breath, like something fishy and spoiled.

Then Spotter's powerful wings were carrying them away, high into the air until the river was just a scribbling twist of water below them, and Longtooth himself looked no larger than a common lizard.

"I owe you one," Max said to Spotter gratefully. "That was way too close!"

Soon after, Max stood in the courtyard of the bug fortress, reporting back to General Barton. The titan beetle listened gravely as Max told the bug commanders all about

General Longtooth and the threat of the coming reptile armada.

"Longtooth," Barton said thoughtfully. "I'm not surprised that evil old creature has stepped in to take Komodo's throne. He tried to take power while Komodo was still alive, you know. But Komodo was too clever for him, and led him into a trap. Longtooth barely got out alive. That's how he got that scar on his nose."

"That's right, General, but we have an invasion on our hands!" said Buzz, getting right to the point as usual. "Clearly the reptiles will try anything to get back onto Bug Island, even with the lava bridge destroyed."

"Then we will fight!" bellowed Barton. "I'm ready. Let them come!"

Some of the bugs cheered, but Webster buried his head in the dirt and put his fore-legs on top of it.

"What are we going to do?" came his muffled voice. "There's a whole armada of crocodiles coming, with an army of lizards on their backs! How are we supposed to fight against a force like that?"

Max patted his spider friend comfortingly. "Don't worry, Webster. I've got an idea."

"Y-you do?"

Max nodded. "General Barton? It's time to put your Goliath beetles to use."

BATTLE PLAN NIAGARA

Twilight slowly fell across Bug Island. Shadows deepened and a chill crept into the air.

Down by Darkmist Lagoon everything was strangely quiet, as if the world was holding its breath. Even the constant roar of Eternity Falls had died down to a whispering gurgle.

Max and Spike crouched in the under-growth near the water's edge. All day long, the bugs had been hard at work. But there was no time to rest. Any moment now, the invaders would be here.

With a whir of wings, Spotter landed close by.

"Are the Goliath beetle divisions in posi-tion?" Max asked her.

"Yes!" Spotter said. "It's all ready, just like you wanted. There's one group up at the top of the waterfall, and another down the river, at its narrowest point."

"Where's Barton?"

"Leading the second group. He's in a pretty good mood."

"I bet he is." Max grinned. "He's finally got something to do. I just hope my plan works, because we've only got one shot at this."

Max looked up at the waterfall. A hastily assembled dam of mud, stones, and thick twigs was blocking off the flow, reducing it to a mere trickle. All the pent-up water must be forming a new, second lagoon up at the top. *Just so long as it stays there for as long as it needs to,* Max thought, *this plan might even work . . .*

"Stay close," he told her. "Is your flying squadron ready?"

"Ready and waiting—hold on, did you hear that?"

Max froze and listened hard. A *chirrup* noise came from the undergrowth, and another one seconds after.

"That's the grasshopper alarm," he whispered. "Enemy inbound. Light them up!"

All across the lagoon, silently hovering fireflies suddenly lit up. Crimson light flooded across the water, clearly revealing the dark shapes of General Longtooth and his fellow crocodiles making their way upstream.

But the crocodile invaders were only half the story. Each one was carrying a whole battalion of common lizards, crowded onto the crocodiles' backs like marauding pirates on a ship.

Just as Max had thought, the crocs were

acting as troop transporters, ferrying lizard soldiers over from Reptile Island. This was a full-on river invasion!

Max rode out on Spike. He stood on the lagoon's shore, watching the crocodiles drift closer and closer to land. The crocodiles' eyes gleamed in the red light from the fireflies, as did the eyes of the hundreds of lizards perched on top of them.

"Well, hello again," Longtooth boomed across the dark water. "I told you I'd be back, and I always keep my promises. Guess you've noticed there's a couple more of us now."

The lizard troops cackled with laughter.

"We don't care how big your force is," Max said. "So you have a few hundred lizards on your side? Big deal. We've got *thousands* of bugs on ours."

Right on cue, more fireflies lit up their bodies. These were on the shores of the lagoon, and the wide ring of light revealed a gigantic army of shield bugs braced to fight, waiting in the undergrowth. More bugs stood alongside them: lean, eager mantises, hulking scorpions, and even the bizarre-looking ant lions.

"All the more for us to eat!" hissed one of the lizards on Longtooth's back. "You thought we were gone for good. You thought you were safe. But you were wrong!"

"Enough talk. Get on that beach and fight!" snarled Longtooth.

The crocodiles splashed up into the

shallows and dragged themselves onto the muddy shore. They lowered their heads like landing ramps. The lizards screeched war cries as they scuttled forward, heading for the bug ranks.

"Battle Bugs, attack!" Max yelled.

The bugs surged forward in a scuttling tide, trampling the undergrowth and flooding over the oncoming lizards. Strength in numbers was the bugs' best hope. For every bug the lizards managed to claw off, a dozen took its place.

Longtooth and the other crocodiles slid back into the water and submerged their bodies. They watched the battle unfold, their eyes glittering above the surface.

Spike grabbed a lizard that was rushing

at him and held it up. While the lizard kicked and struggled in Spike's pincers, he marched it to the edge of the lagoon and flung it in.

Nearby, the other bugs were forcing the lizards back through sheer force of numbers. The lagoon began to fill with floundering, splashing lizards.

General Longtooth watched suspiciously. "The bugs don't seem to be stinging or biting much," he mused. "It seems like they just want to give the lizards a dunking in the lagoon. What's *that* about?"

You're about to find out, Max thought.

Overhead, the enormous form of Dobs the giant dobsonfly zoomed past, carrying an unlucky lizard in his pincers. "BOMBS

AWAY!" he yelled, and dropped the lizard down into the water.

"That's it! Push them into the lagoon!" Max ordered.

Spotter hovered just above him. "Ready, Max?"

"Not yet, Spotter. Just a few more . . ."

Soon, almost all the lizards were forced back into the shallow waters. They crouched there, eyeing the bugs nervously. They'd quickly learned that the bugs wouldn't follow them into the water, so they were safe from further attack.

"Something's up," said General Longtooth. "Lizards, retake that beach. That's an order!"

Max grinned. "Spotter, *now*! Execute battle plan Niagara!"

Longtooth looked puzzled. "Now what in the heck is a Niagara?"

Spotter zoomed up to the waterfall. "Okay, bugs," she bellowed. *"Hit it!"*

On both sides of the dam, groups of Goliath beetles began to move. They heaved their huge bodies against sticks that Max had been very careful to position in just the right places.

There was a low grinding sound as the rocks inside the dam began to shift.

Max crossed his fingers. Building the dam had been a feat of bug engineering, but it was all for nothing if they couldn't demolish it at exactly the right time.

Fresh streams of water burst from the dam. The whole mass sagged in the middle.

Ripples spread out across the lagoon as the waterfall gathered force.

General Longtooth blinked. He'd just noticed he was beginning to drift away from the shore.

Up at the dam, the Goliath beetles were straining at one of the trigger sticks. More and more joined in, but it just wasn't budging.

Spotter flew up high and came back down on a collision course. She yelled a wild, high whoop as she built up speed. In the next moment, she crashed right into the stick, giving it a final wallop and knocking it free.

A rock right at the heart of the dam gave

way, and suddenly, the whole construction collapsed.

Max watched in awe. It was like a chain reaction. A thundering white column of water came down into the lagoon.

The lizards realized what was coming a second too late. They tried to fight their way back onto the shore, but the waves from the waterfall engulfed them.

Max and the Battle Bugs watched as the mighty lizard army was swept away down the river.

CROCODILES, ATTACK!

The bugs cheered as the common lizards were washed away in a foaming tide of river water. The once-proud army went coasting out of the lagoon and away down the river, toward the rapids.

Max could still hear the faint howls and cries of the lizard troops long after they had vanished from sight.

"Phase one complete," he said.

"That's those lizards dealt with," Spike grunted, sounding satisfied. "But I think we've still got problems, little buddy!"

In the center of the lagoon, the crocodiles were still lurking. The water from the waterfall eddied and surged around them, but they were big, powerful reptiles, not like the little lizards. They were strong enough to swim against the flow.

"I should never have sent a bunch of pesky lizards to do a crocodile's job," snarled General Longtooth as the last of his shattered lizard army went tumbling past, legs and tails flailing. He glared at Max. "You led us into a trap."

"I knew we could outsmart you," Max said.

"What did you just say to me?" The crocodile swam furiously toward Max. "I'm gonna snap you up like a crawfish. Crocodiles, attack!"

The group of saltwater crocodiles waded into the shallows and trudged up the shore, plowing right into the bug forces. Max steered Spike out of Longtooth's path.

The crocs laid into the bugs, gnashing their huge jaws and slamming with their clawed feet. The crocs were the biggest reptiles they'd ever faced, with armored skin that was all but impossible to penetrate.

Whole battalions of shield bugs were

flung into the air and fell back down like rain. Scorpions jabbed with their stingers, only to have them glance off the thick crocodile hide. Hornets tried to jab at the crocs' vulnerable eyes, but it was impossible to get near a creature that could snap you out of the air in a split second.

"Don't bother trying to eat them!" Longtooth bellowed to his allies. "Just squish them like the bugs they are!"

The crocodiles laughed mockingly as they heaved themselves forward.

Max turned to look for the dragonfly commander. "It's time for phase two of the plan," he said. "Spotter, I need you!"

"On my way!" shouted the brave dragonfly. She dived down and hovered close, so that Max could climb off Spike's back and onto hers.

With the other dragonflies following, the two of them flew over toward Longtooth, who glanced up at them angrily. He snapped his jaws at Spotter, but she danced easily out of his reach.

The other dragonflies buzzed around the crocodiles' heads, yelling insults and making rude noises. Annoyed, the crocodiles turned from attacking the ground bugs to snapping at the dragonflies, who easily dodged them.

"Nice scar you've got on your nose," Max taunted Longtooth. "Got led into a trap, did you?"

"Get over here!" Again, Longtooth lunged at Max in irritation. Once more, Spotter swerved out of the way.

"If you want me, you'll have to do better than that!" Max jeered.

Moving surprisingly fast for something so huge, Longtooth turned and gave chase. He swam through the water snapping at Spotter and Max, who rocketed away from him just above the surface.

Max glanced to his left and right and saw that the other dragonflies had baited the crocodiles into following them, too. The group rushed out of the lagoon and down the course of the river. Behind came the crocodiles, churning up the water like dark, scaly torpedoes.

"You're going to wish you'd never crossed me!" Longtooth roared.

"Keep going!" Max urged Spotter, who was dipping down toward the water's surface. One of Max's sneakers caught the water.

Spotter put on a fresh burst of speed and veered up into the air again.

Ahead, the river narrowed and the rock walls of Flintfang Gorge loomed up. Max recognized the spot where he'd been trapped earlier.

He looked back and saw that the crocodiles had all splashed down the rapids and into the canyon. They wouldn't be able to climb out quickly. Good.

"Spotter, take us up to Barton," he ordered.

Spotter flew straight up, past the loose, crumbling rock of the canyon walls. She landed next to General Barton, who was peering over the edge of the clifftop.

Behind the general stood thousands of Goliath beetles, each one braced against a massive lump of jagged flint.

Max gave Barton a thumbs-up.

"There's the signal," Barton said with relish. "Goliath beetles, get to work. Shove those stones!"

The Goliath beetles, working together, began to roll the heavy stones to the edge of the cliffs. Down below, the crocodiles snapped and turned in circles, trying to catch the annoying dragonflies.

Max grinned. *The dragonflies are keeping the crocs right where I want them!*

The Goliath beetles pushed and pushed until the first of the stones went tumbling over the cliff. Others followed. They rattled and bumped down the cliff walls, knocking larger chunks of flint loose. The bigger chunks fell like sledgehammers, dislodging even bigger rocks.

Suddenly, the whole of Flintfang Gorge echoed with the rumble and roar of falling rocks. The Goliath beetles had triggered a full-on landslide, and the crocs were at the bottom of it . . .

TURNING TAIL

"Argh!" yelled a crocodile as a sharp flint whacked him on the nose.

"Stand your ground," growled Longtooth as pebbles, stones, and boulders rained down on him. "We can't let them—*argh!*" A heavy lump of flint bounced off the general's flat, scaly head.

The crocodiles ran madly to and fro, but

there was no escaping the stones, and the rockfall just kept on coming. Goliath beetles pushed more stones over the edge, triggering even more rockfalls. The crocs' bodies were soon white with crumbled chalk and piled high with stony debris. They looked as if a backhoe on a building site had emptied gravel over them.

The smallest crocodile had had enough. It turned and fled down the river, away from the chaos. Longtooth snarled angrily at it, but the crocodile wasn't listening.

Suddenly, Longtooth was facing mutiny. His croc commanders all turned tail and fled, away from the hail of stones. However afraid of him they might be, they didn't want to be buried alive.

Only Longtooth was left.

"You haven't seen the last of us, bugs!" he hissed. "We'll be back. Count on it!"

With that, he heaved himself out of the rock pile that had built up around him and waddled away down the river, his clawed feet *slap-slap-slapp*ing on the mud. Max watched him glide away in the water, and punched the air in triumph.

"We'll be ready for you," Max shouted to him. "Count on *that*."

Two nearby Goliath beetles hoisted Max and Spotter onto their backs and set off for the bug camp. Max heard thousands of bug voices cheering as they carried him in victory.

As bugs celebrated in the safety of the camp, Barton leaned over to Max.

"It seems to me that the reptiles will try any way they can to get across the sea and attack us," he said. "In the old days, we could watch the lava bridge. But now we'll have to be alert in all directions."

"They're bound to try the river again," Max said. "It's the easiest way for them to reach our camp." Thinking about the river reminded him of his first sight of Spotter, and gave him an idea.

"Hey, Spotter?" he called. "Why don't you and your fellow dragonflies set up an early warning system along the length of the river? Then if any lizards try and come back that way, we'll be ready for them."

"I'll get right on it!" Spotter replied.

Suddenly, Max felt the hairs prickle on the back of his neck. He knew that feeling all too well—it was the mysterious force of the *Encyclopedia* tugging him back to the human world.

"That's my cue to leave," he said. "Bye, Barton! Bye, Spike! Bye, Webster— whooooa!" Before he could finish his sentence, he was plucked off his feet and dragged up into the spinning, windy tunnel between the worlds.

"That was fast!" he said as he landed back in the cabin at Camp Greenwood. Then he laughed, shook himself, and dashed outside to play with his friends.

Almost no time had passed at all. It was

still the last day of camp, and he could hear Scott, Jamal, and Mark whooping and splashing in the distance.

He ran along the forest path, not slowing down for anything or anyone this time. He jumped off the jetty with a wild yell and landed in the river.

The splash that went up was almost as big as the waterfall flooding the lagoon back on Bug Island . . . but luckily, there were no crocodiles here at camp!

REAL LIFE
BATTLE BUGS!

Australian emperor dragonfly

The Australian emperor dragonfly—also known as the Yellow dragonfly or the Baron dragonfly—is one of the largest dragon-flies in the world. It can grow up to seven centimeters long and have a wing-span of eleven centimeters. As its name suggests, it is found in Australia, over large expanses of fresh water such as ponds and lakes. However, it's also found in New Zealand, New Guinea, parts of Indonesia, and other islands in the Pacific Ocean.

The Emperor dragonfly species is known for its impressive, jewel-like colors: everything from sky blue to emerald green. That's how it received its royal title. However, the Australian emperor dragonfly is usually bright yellow, with a pale to dark brown mottled effect down the length of its body.

The Australian emperor spends most of its life flying quickly across ponds and lakes, defending its territory from rival dragonflies and chasing away any other flying insect that comes too close. Despite the fact that it's been around for about

300 million years—old enough to be around when the dinosaurs lived—individual dragonflies have a short lifespan. Most Australian emperors only live for about six months!

Goliath beetles

Goliath beetles are among the largest beetles in the world—adults can measure up to four inches long. They're not quite as big as the Titan beetle, but they come pretty close! The species is native to Africa and is most often found in the tropical rain forests near the equator.

The females of the species are a dark brown color, but the males are much more striking. They have a bold black-and-white striped pattern on the carapace, which continues down to a hard shell covering its wings. This makes it one of the most distinctive beetles in the forest.

Males have a horn in the shape of the letter Y, which they use to fight their rival beetles. Confrontation can occur over anything from breeding rites to the best spots for feeding. Females have more of a wedge-shaped head, which allows them to dig holes in which they bury their eggs.

MAX'S ADVENTURE CONTINUES!

Turn the page for a special sneak peek!

Max knew he was heading for something gross. He could tell by the smell: a blend of stagnant water, rotten vegetation, and old, black mud. It was a bit like the smells of a well-used soccer field in the rain. Then, suddenly, came the impact: a *squelch* that left him standing in cold, boggy sludge up to his knees.

"Gross!" he yelled as he shook dirt off his hands.

Max took a second to get his breath back, then looked around into the nighttime that enveloped him. This was way darker than night ever seemed at home. He took a step forward, and then hesitated. With this little light to see by, he could easily blunder into a deep bog or pool, and never come out again. Better to take it real slow.

"This is some welcome to Bug Island," he muttered as his eyes slowly adjusted to the dark.

Through the leafy cover overhead, he made out faint stars and a slim crescent of moon. All around lay stretches of black, oily-looking water with patches of firmer ground rising up from it. Reflected stars glimmered in the surface. Farther away into the marsh, a dim blue mist hovered over the water like smoke.

Max decided not to stick around—predators could be anywhere in the dark and he would have no idea. He heaved himself out of the marsh and trudged up to higher, drier ground, leaving a glistening trail of swamp sludge in his wake.

He looked out from the hill, and suddenly he knew where he was. "The Misty Marshes!" he said out loud. I've seen these on the *Encyclopedia* map! That means the jungle is . . . this way!"

He peered into the distance, and sure enough, he thought he could make out the silhouette of trees. "If I can just reach the jungle, I can find the bug camp! As long as Barton hasn't moved it again."

The night air was damp and chilly against his skin. Max was dressed for a day at the park, not a night in the marshes. He zipped up his hoodie and kept moving. The outline of the jungle, even blacker than the sky overhead, loomed in the distance.

Max jumped over yet another soggy spot and noticed a strange depression in the ground. There were more little pockmarks and holes nearby. He paused for a while, trying to figure out what kind of bug could have made them, then shrugged and moved on. The Misty Marshes were beginning to give him the creeps.

He stopped. A light had flashed up ahead.

Max peered into the distance, suddenly alert.

It flashed again.

"What *is* that?"

Although it was just a tiny flicker against the blanketing darkness, Max's hope grew. Only one thing made a light like that—a firefly! And that meant Max wasn't alone out in the dark after all.

Max sprinted toward the light and his grin grew broader as he recognized the glowing insect. It was his trusted friend, the head of the bug underground intelligence network: Glower.

"Hey, Glower!" Max shouted. "I'm glad

to see you! I can hardly see a thing out here!"

"No problem!" came Glower's faint voice shouting back to him. "I'll come to you! Don't go near the . . ." His voice faded away.

"Near the what?" Max hollered, but Glower's words were lost on the night air. Max gritted his teeth and ran on toward Glower's light.

The firefly zoomed toward him. Glower was flying so low he was almost brushing the ground. Suddenly, though, something burst up from one of the dark holes. It was snakelike, reptilian, and moved with a hunched wriggle that made Max feel sick with fear.

"Glower, watch out!" Max shouted.

"Huh?" Glower said.

The reptile twisted around to glare hatefully at Max. He had never seen anything like it before. It had a long, scaly body and a stubby little head, just like a snake. But it also had small, clawed forelimbs, just like a true lizard.

A Mexican worm lizard!

The worm lizard lunged up at Glower, chomping and scrabbling. The firefly darted out of the way, but not quickly enough.

"Another tasty morsel," the worm lizard hissed in delight.

"Max, get out of here!" Glower shouted as the reptile grabbed him by the leg. A quick tussle, a sudden tug—and Glower's light vanished.

JOIN THE RACE!

It's an incredible adventure through the animal kingdom, as kids zip-line, kayak, and scuba dive their way to the finish line! Packed with cool facts about amazing creatures, dangerous habitats, and more!

scholastic.com